CROWN
of
TAILS

KEVIN GREEN

author HOUSE®

AuthorHouse™
1663 Liberty Drive
Bloomington, IN 47403
www.authorhouse.com
Phone: 833-262-8899

Published by AuthorHouse 11/05/2020

ISBN: 978-1-6655-0703-5 (sc)
ISBN: 978-1-6655-0702-8 (e)

Intro
I bring to you the reader
My Crown of Tales.

I started writing this book to improve my life when I had no place to go searching for something greater than myself I had to take a journey inside myself to create happiness and this is part of the information that came to me in my time of need, through a pen that helped create the contents of this book. I wanted to share the stories I've created with the world hoping to entertain and tickle the imagination of the reader. The contents of this book was a great step in the correct direction in a great time of need. I hope this book finds at least one person to help bring greater understanding, peace, love, and happiness to help guide oneself in this great journey called life.

THE STORY OF THE MONKEY IN THE TREE AND THE CAT

Wisemen say that they learned their Kung Fu styles watching other animals in the forest move around bonding together, protecting their life from the other animals in the forest. The monkey being one of the wisest in the forest, lived high in the trees amongst the leaves and the tall branches where all the fruit grew after the rains came. Extremely intelligent, afraid and walking through the forest searching for food and water and friendship the monkey thought. But it was a cat and the monkey remembered what the trees said ??? in his realm would be a friend ???

tree and ??? can't beat me with my Kung Fu, because I climb my tree everyday and eat my own poo! Because I listen to the tree and I train and practice my hand technique to train Kung Fu said the monkey to the cat that fell from the tree.

(Practice makes perfect).

The Story of the Serpent and the Rat

A young serpent just hatched from his egg all alone in the world left to fend for his self, searching to find a place to hide from all the hunters in the forest. And after a few moons had passed the serpent had grow and doubled in size after feeding on little frogs, and crickets to fill his belly. And across the water underneath a fallen tree a mother rat raising her young started to explain why the rats feared the serpent. Mother rat said to her young, the serpent will eat anything it can find because they crawl on their belly, and the rats have to stick together in order to stay safe from the serpent and all of the other hunters in the forest that lie and wait in the shadows. And her young ask their mother why can't we fight the serpent. And the mother rat said, we can't fight the serpent until were big and strong, and told them to remember that a rat can never trust a snake. As the serpent still alone waiting in the shadows to find his next meal, still in shadows away from all the other hunters that prey on others in the forest.

- A female assassin said if you drink shiriken water you will improve your aim and accur - Shiriken water -

Soak the shirikens or stars in water and drink a little of the water while training to throw the shirikens at a target and the shiriken water will improve your aim. This technique works well with wooden objects as well. Practice makes perfect.

STORY

THE LIONS HEAD

12-09-2018

Once upon a time in Africa a small boy was walking through the jungle searching for fruits and berries, hunting for food with only luck and his faithful spear made from harden wood from the trees that surrounded his village caught a monkey in a tree to help feed the people in his village and some fruits and berries while enjoying life and boundties, greatful for the food he had gathered for the day as he continued to talk to the wind, when the small boy heard someone say in the distance beyond the trees in the jungle, run run the lion's coming the lion's coming from villagers nearby. The small boy heard people screaming in pain while the animals of the jungle ran to safety. Help, help the lion's coming, the lion's coming said the villagers as they tried their best to hide from the lion that had found their village hidden from sight to help keep them safe. The lion's coming the lion's coming as the all ran away as the small boy searched to find the village to help the people in the village with his faithful spear. Roar goes the lion. The small boy too far away to

help, cursed life for keeping him from saving the people in the village from the roar of the lion. Finding the village too late to help vowed to kill and eat the lion that had destroyed the peace between man and beast. The small boy vowed to track the lion who had killed the people in the village to the edge of the Earth if he had to. Following the paw prints for many days, and many night sleeping in trees to stay safe while he hunted the lion and finally found the man eating lion in a hole built by hyenas, the small boy cornered the lion while seeking revenge for the people in the village throws his faithful spear and pierces the lions heart after many days and nights of tracking. And after bringing down the lion the small boy skins and cuts the lion's head off at the kneck, leaving the rest of the lions body to rott. And while crying tears of joy, still in pain from the sight of the villagers that were killed and eaten by the lion, the small boy puts the lions hand in a sac made from the skin of the lion and carried the lions head back to his village to eat. Still grieving from the deaths of the villagers that had passed the small boy made it back to his village and added some water from the cleanest river, and some sweet fruit that he had found in the jungle while hunting and a little black magic to a pot he made himself and put the lions head in the pot. And the small boy said to the lions head, I will bring the lions head back to life, just to talk to him and I will eat his eyes so the small boy could see what happened and truely understand why the lion murdered the people of the village. And then the small boy started to chant and cry in the ancient ways, bringing the soul of the lion back to the surface. Then after the small boy finished his chant the small boy started to drink the water inside the pot that held the lions head, consuming

the essence and the soul of the beast that had murdered the people in the village. And as the small boy waited for his curse to work a week and a day went by and the lions head started to move inside the pot. And then the small boy heard the lions head whisper to him in his ear, as the lions head searched for air to breathe underneath the water in the pot. And the lions head asked the small boy, why he had killed the lion and put his head in a pot inside his hut? And the small boy said I hunted the lion and took his head because he had murdered many people in the village many moons ago, when I was at hunting for food and fruit and I have finally my people have been avenged. And the lions head said, why would you kill a king of the jungle for eating the people who kill more than they could ever eat? And the small boy said to the lions head because I am a great hunter and I must protect my village and my people. And the lions head said in the little boys ear, I am the same as you, that's why I came to eat the people who have broken the sacred law of the jungle, and if you were a lion you would do the same to ensure peace and harmony as far as the eyes can see. And the small boy angered by the voices of the lions head ringing inside his head said the lion isn't welcome in our village because the lion comes to eat our people. And the lions head said why would you blame me for eating the meat of the land, when you eat the meat just like me? And the small boy said listening to the voices of the lions head, I'm not the same as you, because I eat the fruit and the monkey and I'm a small boy not a lions head sitting in a pot. And the ground started to shake and the lions head said with anger I came to your village to defend your people from the man eaters as a king of the jungle and if you continue to drink

the water, you will be the same as me. And the small boy started to laugh, and walked up to the pot that held the lions head and started to drink as much of the water in the pot as the small boy as he could. And the grounded started to shake. And the small boy heard the lions head say, I am blind and now I can see so now the man that had murdered the lion, king of the jungle will be the same as me, said the lions head. And the ground started to shake and the winds started to blow pushing down all the bushes and trees that surrounded the small boys hut. And the small boy watched the lions head stand up and turned the small boy into a lion by swelling him whole for killing the lion king of the jungle. Once upon a time.

- <u>Soaking the mouth with milk,</u> increases the health and well being of the mouth teeth, and gums. Also helps to rid the mouth and body of unwanted bugs and parasites. Drinking milk also helps rid the body of gas and bloating, (increasing the health of digestion).
- Passing of gas or flatulence releases great negative energy from the mind and body leaving the mind and body relaxed and at ease. This is a very healthy well to slim to waste and rid toxic gas from the mind and body.

(The Sand Eater)

• Wisemen say eating a spoon full of sand whenever possible will increase ones inner strengths, (like bathing in sand.)

(After visiting the land of the mists) Ga was told to search and find the madam of Voo to learn the ancient ways of voodoo in order for Ga to cast a spell on the tribe of the white lions to break through their defenses to save Ga's people from slavery and torture.

Curing sore muscles

Great helpful medicine for muscle fatigue, use analgesic gel or something that contains analgesic gel with menthol to rid the body of muscle fatigue by massaging the analgesic gel firmly into the muscles without damaging the muscle fibers, massaging the muscles with analgesic gel, one coat at a time will allow the body to rid the body of muscle fatigue internal and external pests and parasites, and also the analgesic gel helps rid the ???

See the moon raise and the sun fall.
I believe
I sing for Africa.
I hope you hear the
words I sing
Sing for freedom
Sing for peace
Sing for Africa.
I hope when you think of me
my friend,
I hope you think of Africa.
I left this message to you
as I express the song I sing.

KG

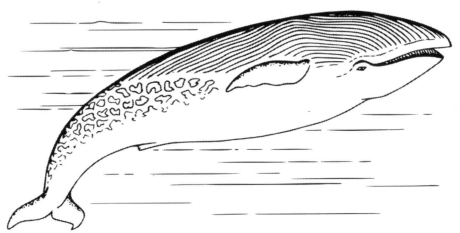

STORY

THE TIGER AND THE WHALE

One day a tiger was walking on the shore, hoping to find something to eat. And while staring at the waves of the ocean crash onto the sand on the beach. When all of a sudden, started to spray into the air, water coming from a whale catching fish in the swallows. The tiger asked the whale, if the whale would be nice enough to share some of his fish with him. The tiger still sore and hungry from walking searching for something to eat. The whale replied, I will share some of my fish with you, if you swim out to me, and climb into my mouth. The tiger still hungry and tired from hunting with no luck in sight, says to the whale. I haven't eaten in seven days and then shook the dry sand off of his coat and then agreed to swim out to the whale to eat some fish, to cure his hunger for the day. The whale then opened his mouth as wide as the whale could manage. After watching the whale open his mouth the tiger still on shore, jumped into the surf and swam all the way to the opened mouth of the whale, still waiting in the swallows. Once the tiger arrived at the mouth of the whale, the tiger then jumps into the

whales mouth, to eat some fish. And as soon as the tiger was all the way in the whales mouth, the whale shut his jaws imprisoning the tiger inside the mouth of the whale. The tiger now inside the belly of the beast, hears the whale laughing as the whale says, welcome now you can eat all the fish you can eat as the whale heads to the bottom of the sea, to finish his meal for the day. The tiger scared, hungry, and faced with danger the tiger decides to eat his way out of the belly of the beast, as the whale continues to laugh on his way to the bottom of the sea. The tiger now in the stomach of the whale, bites the belly of the whale and the tiger heard the whale you're not suppose to eat me, you're in my belly. And the tiger told the whale, he would stop biting the whale if the whale opened his mouth to let the tiger out, and the whale agreed to open his mouth to release the tiger from imprisonment inside the belly of the whale. And after the whale reached the surface once more to release the tiger. The whale opens his mouth and the tiger now free from the belly of the whale, jumps safely back into the sea to swim back to shore. Left to find for himself and find his own food. Still tired and hungry the tiger learns never to jump into the belly of the beast.

KG

STORY

YOUNG LITTLE INDIAN BOY

Turning through these pages of the book of fortune and stopping at a very special story I leave for you. A tale of a young Indian boy and frog that calls itself the Devil. Once upon a time in a small village in the middle of the county a young Indian boy opens his eyes with a smile as the sunshine starts to burn from brightness of day as the young little Indian boy opens his ears and hears his mother call and says good morning. Rise and shine as the young Indian boy so hungry and ready to start the day, and begins his early morning chores for his mother and his village. So the young Indian boy says good morning to his mother and heads as site and races, to his pales for water and rubs on the special tonic that his father gave him to keep him safe from harm so he and his family can eat and drink before the young boy's father learns to hunt for their next meal to keep their family feed. And soon after picking of his pales for water the young Indian boy starts to kick up and hears a frog in throat ribbit goes the frog over and over again as the young Indian boy continues to kick up. And the little Indian boy now heading back

to his village with the water his mother and family needed for their morning meal. Starts to hear a voice whisper and told boy story in his ear as the young Indian boy makes it back to his village the voice from the frog inside his throat stops. Surprise and eager to explain what the little boy heard from the frog in his throat. The little Indian boy tells his mother he had something real important to tell her and it couldn't wait and the little Indian boy's mother says okay son what is it. And the little boy says I finished with my chores for the day and I heard a voice in my throat that started to ribbit and said that she was a frog in my throat called the Devil and the Devil said she was a frog eating my food from inside my throat absorbing my strength searching for the wicked, taking the souls of the unfortunate ones.

And the little Indian boy frightened and disturbed with what her son had said. Quickly leaves her hut and takes her son to the village witch doctor and explains to their medicine man and their village medicine man says to the little boy (what did the frog do after he spoke to you) and the little Indian boy said the Devil had to leave for feasting on the food of the Gods. And the medicine man of their village kindly explains to the little Indian boy and the little Indian boys mother that the little Indian boy has now become a man and has passed his test of manhood. And will be granted a seat next to his father at their nightly feast. And the little Indian boy proudly smiles and nods and asks the village medicine man how did the frog end up in his throat, and the medicine man replies and explains to the young boy and the little boys mother that we have in the village are hunted by frogs and all things we can't always see with the naked

eye because the slip into your throat after biting and injecting toxin, to judge their prey. The elders and other wise men say when the frogs of the forest eat enough bugs and spiders they become strong enough to test ones soul after gaining the gift of invisibility, searching for immortality, feeding on the appetite of man as they continue to find a reason to suck on the souls of mankind. Grateful to hear the news the little Indian boy mother smile with joy and hugs her son, for getting rid of the Devil. As they begin their journey back to their hut to once again begin their morning meal. The little Indian boys mother hugs her husband as the little Indian boy tells his father the good news and how he beat the Devil.

(I have been using like treatment for the past two and a half years and I have been using emu oil for the past year, and this is my story to you).

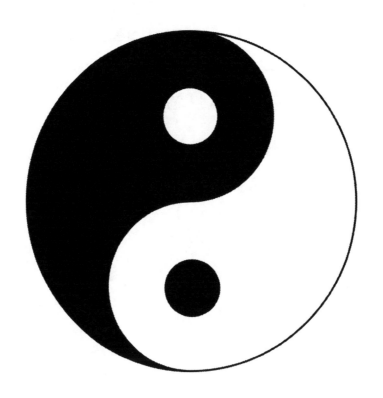

DEEP MEDITATION

A wise man once said to always remember that the Gods and Devils of the world create balance to create a realm safe enough to train so life would be safe enough to follow our own path to righteousness.

Remember we the chosen ones make it safe so we don't have to fight.

Train and be well, and may God Bless us all!!!

Kevin Green

May-07-2020

STORY

TRAPPED A MONKEY IN A CAGE

Running for his peace of mind and safety and his life in fear of being caught by the hunter a monkey was far ahead of the pack of dogs chasing him through the forest and was shared by the hunters trap. Shocked and frightened the monkey still dangling from a rope with a huge sees the hunter approach through the trees as the monkey feels the poison from the hunters blow dot pierces the monkeys skin. Hours after the innsodent the monkey still shakened by the effects from the poison from the dart from the hunter, the monkey opens his eyes and is shocked by the sight of being inside the mans village, trapped inside a cage. As the hunter walks passed the monkey yells (let me go). Shocked by the translation and language of the animal the hunter still shocked by the fact he heard a monkey talk says no I have to feed my family, I can't afford to waste the meat. And walks away and one of the men in the village fell to the ground and died. Everyone in the village in disbelief crying for help from their local witch doctor. The monkey again yells (let me go) as

31

another man in the village falls, face first into the dirt. (Let me go the monkey says) Crying begging for his freedom in fear of losing his life (let me go) yells the monkey as another falls and lands onto a plane of earth (let me go) yells the monkey. Frighten shedding tears for his falling the hunters says why me. And the monkey says you were the one to trap me if you let me go and set me free I will leave your village and your people will be safe from harm. If you and your people promise to never hunter me again the monkey says. Deep inside the forest deep in the mans village surrounded by the wind and the trees of the forest the hunter agrees to the terms and conditions and sets the monkey free and as promised the monkey was never seen again, and all the people in the village lived happily ever after.

KG

STORY

THE KING AND THE FOX

R unning for his life a fox in fear of losing his life after being hunted trice in fear of losing his life is caught by the share form the trap of the hunter, please let me go, please let me go. The fox says please let me go!!! (I was so ahead of the pack) says the fox trapped and snared by the snar and rope of the hunter. As the king says I caught you.

Shocked in fear of being skinned alive still hanging from a rope trapped by a nose the fox sees the king approach through the trees of the forest as the poison from the dart of the king goes into effect. Numb from the toxin. The fox opens his eyes shocked by the sight of the king and his men. Let me go let me go, let me go, let me go says the fox.

Let me go

Let me go

Let me go

Let me go ōō ōō ōō ōō ōōōō

As the king walks passed

- (Let me go) says the fox

Shocked by the words of the fox

Shocked by the vision of intelligence

Shocked by the translation of language

Shocked by the fact one witness an animal talk

The king says no I can't waste a pelt, I need the fur to stay warm a night.

I need your fur, it wasn't warm enough to sleep by candle light.

Let me go

Let me go

Let me go

Let me go ōō ōō ōō ōōōō

Says the fox in fear of his life and being skinned alive

(Let me go)

I need to feed my family

I need to stay health

I need to stay fit

Says the king in front of his country's men

(Let me go) says the fox

I can't afford to waste the meat says the king in front of country

Let me go

Let me go

Let me go

Let me go (ōō ōō ōō) ōōōōōō

Let me go says the fox to his majesty

Let me go to his men

Let me go to his country's men

Please (Let me go) says the fox.

As the king walks away

Watching day after day of his majesty knights fade away

Will you ever let me go

Let me go

Let me go

Let me go ōō ōō

Says the fox

As the king walks away as one of the Kings men falls

Let me go oh oh

Let me go

Shocked in disbelief

The king

The king says

No!!!

Let me go

Let me go

Let me go

Let me go!!!

As another man falls and turns to stone

Let me go

Let me go

Let me go

Let me go

Says the fox to the king begging for his freedom in fear of being skinned alive.

And the king says no

As another one of the kings men falls from his post and turns to ash

Why me, why me says the king to the fox.

And the fox says, if you let me go and set me free, you and your countries men will be safe from harm and no more of your people will fall and the king releases the fox and the king and his countries men lived happily ever after.

KG

- <u>Remember</u> we don't eat the bat, the bat taught me they are <u>more than smart</u> enough to be a friend and they bite us sometimes and eat fruit in order to be a friend, and they don't want men to die. So they deserve respect from me.

God Bless!! ☺

RIP in peace my friend Jon B. its 2020 and I
still love you my friend God Bless!!! ☺
KG
I love you Grand Ma and family may I ago one day rest in peace.
KG

Printed in the United States
By Bookmasters